Smythe Gambrell Library

Presented by
Eric and Ann Liu
in honor of our daughter,
Christine Joy Liu

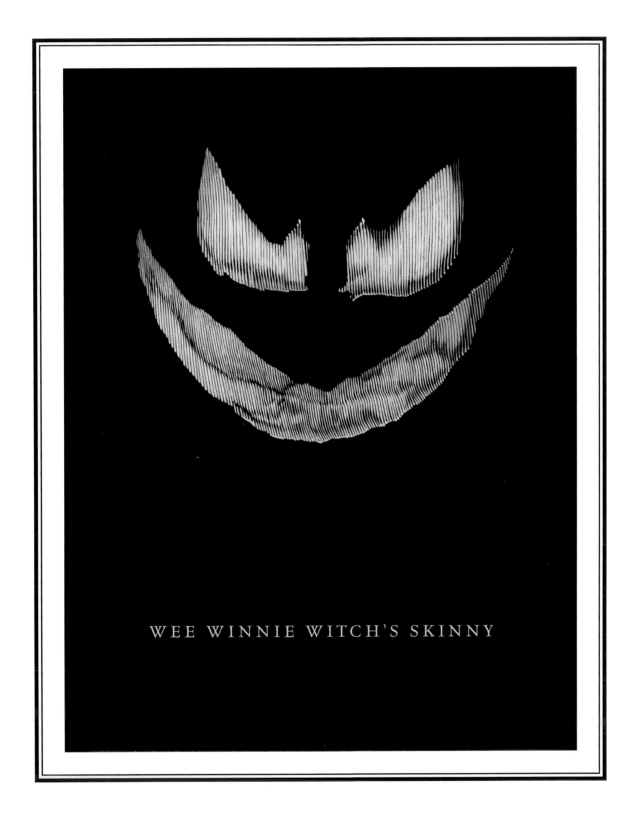

WEE WINNIE WITCH'S SKINNY

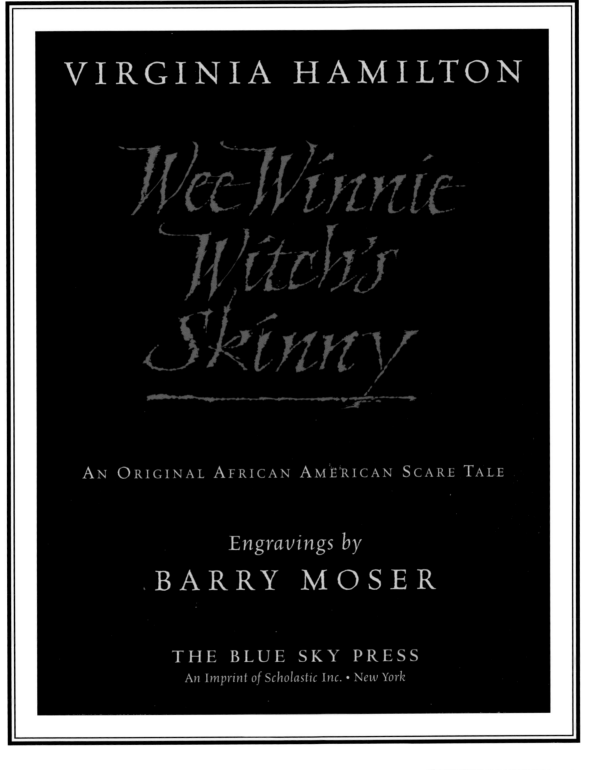

VIRGINIA HAMILTON

Wee Winnie Witch's Skinny

AN ORIGINAL AFRICAN AMERICAN SCARE TALE

Engravings by
BARRY MOSER

THE BLUE SKY PRESS
An Imprint of Scholastic Inc. • New York

Carefully, James Lee drew a black cat wearing a pointy black hat and riding on a broomstick. "I know a lot about witches. I do!" James Lee told his brother, Will. "You better stay away from owls and gnats and cats, too," James Lee warned his little brother. "Cats know the most about witches. Uncle Big Anthony said so." They lived next door to Uncle Big Anthony's house.

"See, Uncle Big Anthony put a gnat in a bottle with the lid on tight," James Lee said. "And, *poof!* The gnat was gone. A teeny witch was in there. And, *whoo-whoo!* An owl hooted, and the witch was gone!" He grinned at Will. Will shivered.

One day, James Lee saw a black cat fall out of a sassafras tree on to Uncle Big Anthony. It held on tight. Uncle Big Anthony couldn't shake off that black cat for anything! He ran. He stopped short. He hollered loud. He slapped at it. But nothing could shake that cat off him.

James Lee tried to sneak up on Uncle Big Anthony to help him. He got close enough to reach for the cat. But the cat arched its back and hissed at him. Its yellow eyes scared him. James Lee ran home to tell his mama.

"A Wee Winnie must be after Uncle Big Anthony," said James Lee's Mama Jo. Wee Winnie was a name she used to make a witch sound small. "Stay away from your Uncle Big Anthony for a while," Mama Jo warned James Lee and Will.

But James Lee always played where he thought Uncle Big Anthony might walk by. He and Will and a whole bunch of boys sat under the sassy trees, resting from standing on each other's shoulders. They'd been forming a ladder to reach the sky, with little Will at the top of it.

All a-sudden, here comes Uncle Big Anthony. He looked like he was dragging himself along. Cat claws had torn his shirt. There were mean scratches on his face and neck.

"Whew-wheee!" James Lee whispered as Uncle Big Anthony limped on by.

Big and jolly Uncle Anthony was looking smaller and sad. There was a scratch in the corner of his mouth where a cat-witch Winnie must've tried to bridle him.

One crisp night of a full yellow moon, James Lee saw Wee Winnie come for Uncle Big Anthony. Uncle Big Anthony had been boxing the moonglow to keep up his nerve. Wee Winnie Witch came creeping like a cat. She changed from a black cat to a thin witch. And she floated through the back door of Uncle Big Anthony's house.

James Lee whispered to Will, "Wee Winnie's after our Uncle Big Anthony!"

The Wee Winnie slowly turned and looked over at James Lee. She must've heard him. She took off her bald head and swung it from side to side in Uncle Big Anthony's window! Her yellow eyes glowed, like the triangles in a candlelit pumpkin. James Lee dived under the covers where Will was. They stayed scrunched together all night.

The next morning, James Lee followed Mama Jo over to Uncle Big Anthony's house. They found him in the hall closet. He refused to come out. What James Lee could see of his uncle's hair was braided into a bridle. That day and all week long, Uncle Big Anthony stayed home sick.

James Lee's Mama Jo sent Uncle Big Anthony sassafras tea and buttermilk biscuits. But weeks passed, and his uncle got lean and bent-over tired. He looked like some about-gone, Uncle Shrunken Anthony. Folks wouldn't pay him respect on Sunday. All of his many children—Sabeen, Simon, Simmony, Rosie, and all the rest—had left home at the first sign of Wee Winnie.

One night, Uncle Big Anthony's wife, Aunt Bea Anna, went running over to her Mama Granny's house, just down the road. Mama Granny said to her, "You stay right here. I'll be over to your house in a short minute."

Mama Granny was a far-seer who could read the future and the past. She could handle any Wee Winnie Witch. Mama Granny took up her cane and her spice-hot pepper witch-be-gone potion, and she made her way over to Uncle Big Anthony's.

James Lee and Will sat in the dark of their bedroom watching Uncle Big Anthony's house. They could hear him blowing and puffing just like a sheepdog. Then, Wee Winnie Witch glided in. "Mama Granny is almost there!" James Lee

whispered to Will. "She'll put a stop to Wee Winnie! Hurry, Mama Granny!"

The night fell down dark, with a golden moon rising. The Wee Winnie was ready for her night ride. In spite of himself, James Lee couldn't wait to see what would happen. Lo and behold, he and Will saw the Wee Winnie go inside.

"Look!" he told Will. "Wee Winnie Witch is taking off her skin! She's hanging it up on the wall next to Uncle Big Anthony's overalls!"

James Lee couldn't believe his eyes. He opened the window to see better. He saw skinless Wee Winnie take hold of Uncle Big Anthony in his nightshirt. And she put the bridle bit in his mouth. She held on to Uncle Big Anthony's braided hair. The witch rode on Uncle Big Anthony's back, right out the front door.

James Lee saw it all. Will saw nothing; he had his eyes tight shut. Wee Winnie Witch rode Uncle Big Anthony twice around his own house. Then, she galloped him over to James Lee's home!

Before James Lee could move, Wee Winnie snatched him right out of the window. She put him in front of her on Uncle Horse Anthony's back. James Lee held on to Uncle Big Anthony's nightshirt for dear life. And he hollered for his family: "Help! Mama, Papa, help me!"

James Lee saw his mama and papa and Will run outside. All of the folks came rushing out of their houses. And it seemed like the folks were getting small! Something about that made

him grin. When he was way up above the sassy trees, James Lee waved at everybody.

The three flyers climbed a night breeze up toward the harvest moon. Uncle Horse Anthony neighed. Wee Winnie Witch cackled and shook the stars. James Lee gazed far below. All of the folks' startled eyes had become like bright sparkles of pumpkin light.

And down below, Mama Granny walked inside Uncle Big Anthony's house. She looked all around.

"They're gone," a neighbor, Naydelle, said, following Mama Granny. "Wee Winnie left her skin behind. And she's taken James Lee, too."

"They'll be back," Mama Granny said. She put down her cane and took the lid off her hot

potion sauce pot. She reached into it now and spooned her spice-hot pepper oil into the Wee Witch's skin hanging there on the wall.

"Let's skedaddle!" she told Naydelle when she had finished. They got out of there as Wee Winnie Witch, Uncle Horse Anthony, and James Lee came in sight.

Wee Winnie rode in. Uncle Big Anthony fell on his bed. James Lee hit the wall and hugged it as tight as wallpaper.

"I'll be back for you both in two nights!" Wee Winnie screeched at them. She took her thin skin down and slipped it on. "Hey, now," said the witch. "Skin?" She started wiggling and turning in her skin. "Skinny, you feel all tight! What's a-wrong with you? Say, now!"

"Peel me off. Strip me off," Skinny said in a fizzley voice.

Winnie Witch tried taking her skin off, but it stuck to her. She moaned and shouted, "Skinny, don't you know Big Witch? Get off of me! Don't you know me, Skinny?"

That skinny was so peppery hot it couldn't talk anymore. It squeezed and squeezed until it took Wee Winnie's breath right out of her. It shriveled her up. She fell to pieces on the floor. Now the Wee Winnie was no more than a bunch of dried-up, skinny leftovers.

James Lee saw it all. He tore himself from the wall and ran out of there. He couldn't wait to tell Will and everybody.

That was how Uncle Big Anthony and

James Lee got free of Wee Winnie Witch. Mama Granny sure did the job.

"What'd'ya think of that?" James Lee asked Will.

"I don't much care for witches," Will said. "I don't believe in them much, either. You probably were dreaming." But he made James Lee keep their bedroom window closed on nights of the harvest moon.

Mama Granny sprinkled secret potion water around the house for seven days. She chanted seven times, "Remove yourself from here! Remove yourself from here!" She and Mama Jo swept up the dry scraps of Wee Winnie Witch's skinny. They burned them in the fireplace and let the smoke carry the ashes away.

James Lee sat with Uncle Big Anthony until Aunt Bea Anna and the children came home. Uncle Big Anthony went back to work the next day.

"He's the best Uncle Big Anthony, just like always," James Lee told Will. "He'll be his old self in no time."

Uncle Big Anthony grew stronger every day. There was only one thing that stayed different about him. He always carried a flyswatter. He smacked his back with it whenever he passed along the sassy trees. That's how James Lee knew when Uncle Big Anthony was coming. "You can hear him splat-swatting with the flyswatter," said James Lee, "in case of black cats."

"Is that the truth?" asked Will. "I would think he'd rather swat flies."

"I wouldn't lie," James Lee said, "so don't you think."

He told everybody about his night-air ride on the back of Uncle Big Anthony. His Uncle Big Anthony said he didn't remember a thing. Still, James Lee told about Wee Winnie Witch's skinny to all the folks.

"I don't ever want to see a skinny again," James Lee told them. "But that night-air ride up to the twinkling stars? Whew-wheee!" His face lit up like moonglow.

Folks begged James Lee to tell the whole tale again. A hundred times, and every Halloween, James Lee did.

ABOUT THIS BOOK

THE scare tale in this book was written by Virginia Hamilton (1936–2002) several years before her death. Ms. Hamilton's exhaustive research over the years led her to find a vast number of witch beliefs in black folklore, including tales of a witch hanging up her skin, which are widespread in Africa, America, and the Bahamas. Witches were commonly thought to ride people, using braided hair as a bridle. Told with the same enthusiasm and intent as a traditional Halloween ghost story, *Wee Winnie Witch's Skinny* is an original work of fiction, and all of Ms. Hamilton's corrections and revisions are included.

Ms. Hamilton was delighted when Barry Moser agreed to illustrate the book with colored wood engravings.

The images in this book are dedicated with love and admiration
to the memory of
VIRGINIA HAMILTON,
wonderful person, splendid writer, good friend.
Her absence leaves the world less rich.
B.M.

THE BLUE SKY PRESS